MATT CHRISTOPHER

Football Jokes
and
Riddles

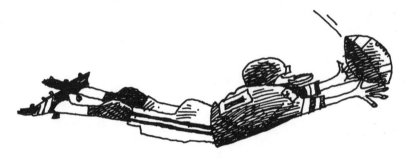

Illustrated by
Larry Johnson

Little, Brown and Company
Boston   New York   Toronto   London

First Edition

Library of Congress Cataloging-in-Publication Data

Christopher, Matt.
    Football jokes and riddles / Matt Christopher ; illustrated by Larry Johnson. — 1st ed.
      p. cm.
    Summary: A collection of anecdotes, jokes, and riddles about the game of football.
    ISBN 0-316-14197-6
    1. Football — Juvenile humor. 2. Riddles, Juvenile. [1. Football — Wit and humor. 2. Jokes. 3. Riddles.] I. Johnson, Larry, ill. II. Title.
GV950.7.C57 1997
796.332'02 — dc21   97-4498

10 9 8 7 6 5 4 3 2 1

COM-MO

Published simultaneously in Canada by
Little, Brown & Company (Canada) Limited

Printed in the United States of America

To my brother, Mike, with a bushel of love and laughs   *— M. C.*

To my family, who deceived me into thinking I was funnier than I am   *— L. J.*

Quarterback: My dog really knows how to play football.

Center: I don't believe it. Prove it!

Quarterback: OK. Fido, who are the guys in the black-and-white shirts on the field?

Fido: Ref! Ref! Ref!

Fan #1: Does water always come through the dome roof like this?

Fan #2: Only when it rains!

Quarterback: I passed your house this morning.

Wide Receiver: Wow! You did? What an arm!

Fan #1: Which NFL receiver can jump higher than a house?

Fan #2: All of them. Houses can't jump!

A Little Traveling Music, Please, Or Try to Get a Handle on It

In the 1890s, the Harvard College football team thought of a unique way to protect the ballcarrier. They sewed suitcase handles onto their uniforms so that offensive players could grasp nearby teammates and create a moving chain of blockers!

Hidden Talent

Auburn University coach John Heisman, for whom the Heisman Trophy is named, was once asked by a player if it was against the rules to hide the football. Heisman answered that it was not, but the question did give him an idea. In a game against Vanderbilt in 1895, he instructed his player to hide the ball under his jersey. The play went fifty yards for a touchdown!

Go, "Faded Maroons"?

The Arizona Cardinals started out as a Chicago amateur team in 1899. In 1901, the team founder, Chris O'Brien, bought used maroon jerseys for his players. The jerseys soon faded to a color O'Brien described as "cardinal red"; hence he dubbed the team the Cardinals. Now, if the jerseys had been brand new, would he have called the team the "New Jerseys"?

All Swimming Team

Ricky Watters

James Brooks

Carnell Lake

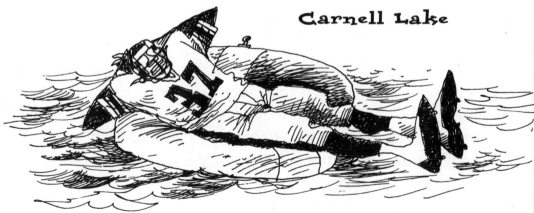

Hampton Pool

Gerald Tubbs

Bob Waterfield

What four letters can stop a quarterback sneak?

O, I C U!

Why was Cinderella such
a poor football player?
She had a pumpkin
for a coach!

Why was Cinderella thrown off the football team?
Because she ran away from the ball!

What the Refs Say

Intentional grounding of pass

Interference with forward pass
or fair catch

Illegal substitution or too many men
on the field

Unsportsmanlike conduct

Illegal contact

What the Players Hear

You do the hokey-pokey, and
you turn yourself around...

Pat-a-cake, pat-a-cake...

Heads, shoulders, knees and toes,
knees and toes . . .

I can fly! Really, I can!

Stop! Please run between
the white lines!

Go Home and Sleep on It,
Or a Dummy at Yale!

One of football's most inventive coaches was Amos
Alonzo Stagg. While a student at Yale in the late 1800s,
he noticed that players were having a hard time learn-
ing to tackle below the waist. So he rolled up a mattress
and hung it from the ceiling. Then he placed another
mattress under it. Thus was born football's first tackling
dummy.

Grab Him by the Horns!

In 1948, Los Angeles Rams halfback Frank Gehrke
painted horns on his team's helmets — the first helmet
emblem in professional football. It's a good thing his
logo design wasn't three-dimensional!

By Special Order of the President

In the early days of football, players could run with the ball but not pass it. Defensive players showed no mercy when attacking the offense, and the ball handlers often wound up at the bottom of a bone-crushing pileup! In fact, in 1906, President Theodore Roosevelt threatened to ban football unless colleges made the game less dangerous. At last, teams were allowed to throw the ball. The first coach to call a pass play was St. Louis University's Eddie Cochems, in 1906. That first pass was incomplete, but Cochem's team went on to a 11–0 record and outscored their opponents 407–11!

Coach: I can't believe you fumbled again!

Fullback: Why not? I've been practicing all day!

Reporter: Did the game have a happy ending?

Coach: Yes, everybody was happy when it ended!

Wide Receiver: What's the best way to catch a ball?

Coach: Have someone throw it to you!

Linebacker: Is it better to play football on a full or empty stomach?

Coach: It's better to play on a field!

Reporter: What's the hardest thing about being tackled?

Fullback: The ground!

All Transportation Team

Elroy
"Crazylegs"
Hirsch

Joe Carr

James Jett

Tank Younger

Night Train Lane

Alan
"The Horse"
Ameche

Raghib "Rocket" Ismail

What runs around the field but does not move?
The out-of-bounds marker!

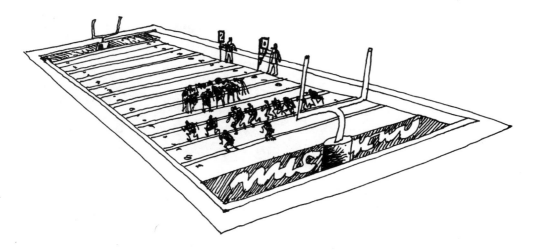

What is green, has three hundred feet, and white stripes?
A football field!

Why is it easy to draw on a football field?
Because there is a marker every five yards!

Why was the quarterback laughing on the sidelines?
He left the game in stitches!

Why did the coach cross
the road?
To get his quarterback!

Bull Run, or Footbull

Mark Gastineau, a defensive end with the New York Jets in the 1980s, was chosen to play in the annual Pro Bowl game in Hawaii. While walking down a Honolulu street, Gastineau unexpectedly ran into something resembling a hard-nosed fullback: a bull, which had escaped from a local zoo! Never one to avoid a challenge, Gastineau wrestled the animal and tackled it. Perhaps he thought the Pro Bowl (or Pro Bull!) had started early!

Oops! Or Pushing up Daisies

In the fifth round of the 1996 spring draft, the Montreal
Alouettes of the Canadian Football League chose a
defensive end who they felt showed a lot of promise.
Imagine how they felt when they found out that this
player had died in December of 1995! In fact, this was
the second time in a year that the CFL had drafted a dead
player! The chairman of the CFL had this to say on the
drafting policies of his league: "I would think that the
first qualification they may want to come up with is that
the person is alive."

The Collector

Since his first pro season in 1990, star running back Emmitt Smith of the Dallas Cowboys has kept every football he's scored a touchdown with. Through the 1995 season, he had already scored 118 touchdowns! He keeps most of the footballs in his card shop in Pensacola, Florida, and some he gives to special friends.

Just Point Me in the Right Direction!

Pro Bowl defensive end Jim Marshall of the Minnesota Vikings didn't have his best day on October 25, 1964. After picking up a fumble, he raced sixty yards to the goal line. He heard screaming and yelling from the crowd and tossed the ball up in the air. Then a 49er ran up and hugged him. Marshall wondered why until he realized he had just crossed the *49er* goal line! The play was ruled a safety — two points for the 49ers — but luckily for Marshall, the Vikings were still able to win the game.

Bill Me Later!

When the Buffalo Bills run out onto the field just before a game, star running back Thurman Thomas is still hanging back in the locker room. Is Thurman nervous? Nope—just superstitious! He always has to be the second-to-last player to leave the locker room so he can say what he says before each game: "Last one out, turn out the lights."

All Hospital Team

Troy Aikman

Ken Payne

Eric Hurt

Leon Hart

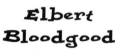

Tom Doctor

Elbert
Bloodgood

What the Refs Say

Illegal forward pass

Loss of down

Offside, encroaching, or neutral zone infraction

Ineligible receiver or ineligible member of kicking team downfield

Uncatchable forward pass

What the Players Hear

My fingers aren't crossed — honest!

Now, if I only had a hammock!

My pants keep falling down!

Look — I can touch my head *and* chew gum at the same time!

And next year I hope to be *this* tall!

Coach: That linebacker had nine sacks!

Trainer: I know. He can barely move!

Fan #1: Did you know that when a lineman slams his man down, it's called a "pancake"?

Fan #2: How waffle!

Reporter: Why is the linebacker sitting on the bench?

Coach: Because he'd take up too much room if he were lying down!

Coach: What's wrong with that player?

Trainer: Oh, that's the *full*back. He ate too much before the game.

All Flower Team

Larry Flowers

Joe Rose

Ron Gardin

Bob
Lilly

Frank
Seeds

Frank
Budd

Where do they play?
The Rose Bowl!

Kitchen Football,
Or Movers and (Salt)Shakers!

Cincinnati Bengals quarterback Jeff Blake played high school football in Sanford, Florida. His dad was the coach, and football practice often carried over to dinnertime at home. With a saltshaker as strong safety, a pepper grinder as weak safety, and water glasses as linebackers, Coach Blake would try to discuss a play with his son at the kitchen table. But Jeff had only one thing to say: "Dad, can we just eat?"

Did You Want Anchovies on That?

In 1986, back in the days of instant replay, Cardinals quarterback Neil Lomax thought the officials were taking an awfully long time to study the replay on a touchdown pass he had just thrown. His response? "I thought they were ordering a pizza!"

And Now for My Next Trick...

In a 1994 game, Tampa Bay Buccaneers linebacker Demetrius DuBose had a very long day chasing Barry Sanders of the Detroit Lions. Sanders ran for 166 yards and disappeared from DuBose's grasp all game. All a tired DuBose could say about Sanders was "He's like Houdini!"

What the Refs Say

Delay of game, illegal substitution, or excess time out

Crawling, interlocking interference, pushing, or helping runner

Player disqualified

Tripping

What the Players Hear

Watch me pull a rabbit out my sleeve!

Won't somebody please believe me!

Can I get a ride home after the game?

Curtsy to your partner!

In what country is it impossible to win a football game?
Thailand!

What is gray, has a trunk, and flies through the air?
An elepunt!

How do you get a down in football?
You don't. You get down from a duck!

Why was the kicker scared after he kicked the ball?

He hit the ghoulpost!

What do you call a ghost sitting in the stands?

A spooktater!

All Haircut Team

Brenton Bangs

Rudolph Barber

Curly Lambeau

Dana Stubblefield

Morris
"Red"
Badgro

Big Daddy
Lipscomb

Herbert
Straight

Ed Beard

What the Refs Say

Penalty refused, incomplete pass, play over, or missed goal

Personal foul

Holding

Illegal use of hands, arms, or body

Illegal motion at snap

What the Players Hear

SAFE!
(Oops, wrong sport!)

Ow! That hurts every time I do that!

Don't worry—
I'm just checking my pulse!

You know, 3 + 2 really is 5!

You must be this tall to ride the
roller coaster!

Get the Message?

To pump himself up before a game, NFL defensive back Andre Waters would write a note to himself with a phrase such as "Be strong today!" But he didn't write it on paper. He wrote it on a piece of tape and then stuck it on his forehead! He only ran into a problem — and into other players — when he tried to read it during a game!

A Moooving Experience

How desperate are people for Super Bowl tickets? For the 1995 Super Bowl between Dallas and Pittsburgh in Tempe, Arizona, a Phoenix radio station offered a pair of tickets to a deserving fan. But there was a catch: The fan had to be willing to dive headfirst into two thousand pounds of cow manure! Fred Flores of Gilbert, Arizona, thought that was a small price to pay and gladly took the plunge.

Sesame Strut

All-Pro safety Merton Hanks of the San Francisco 49ers is known for his victory celebration dance in the locker room after a game. He does an exaggerated strut with his neck bobbing up and down like a pogo stick. His inspiration for the dance? Watching Bert's pigeon dance on *Sesame Street* with his daughter Maya!

All Tree Team

Forrest
Gregg

Stump
Mitchell

Mel
Branch

Donald
Oakes

Bobby
Maples

Zefross
Moss

Nice catch!